Don't Go!

STORY AND PICTURES BY

Jane Breskin Zalben

Clarion Books ▥ New York

Clarion Books
a Houghton Mifflin Company imprint
215 Park Avenue South, New York, NY 10003
Copyright © 2001 by Jane Breskin Zalben
Editor's Note copyright © 2001 by Clarion Books
The illustrations were executed in pen and watercolor.
The text was set in 18-point Venetian.
For information about permission to reproduce selections from this book,
write to Permissions, Houghton Mifflin Company,
215 Park Avenue South, New York, NY 10003.
www.houghtonmifflinbooks.com
Printed in Hong Kong.
Library of Congress Cataloging-in-Publication Data
Zalben, Jane Breskin.
Don't go! / story and pictures by Jane Breskin Zalben.
p. cm.
Summary: On the first day of preschool, Daniel gradually overcomes his nervousness as he plays
in the sandbox, collects leaves, and bakes cookies. Includes tips for parents on getting ready for
preschool and a recipe for pumpkin cookies.
ISBN 0-618-07250-0
[1. First day of school—Fiction. 2. Nursery schools—Fiction. 3. Schools—Fiction.] I. Title.
PZ7.Z254 Do 2001
[E]—dc21   00-065796
SCP 10 9 8 7 6 5 4 3 2 1

To our three sons—

To Michele Coppola's son, Daniel,

for inspiration

and

to my two sons,

Jonathan and Alexander,

whom I love and respect more than words can say.

It was the first day of preschool.
Daniel's mother said, "Time to go."
She packed his lunch and a change of clothes.
Daniel took his stuffed dog
and grabbed his mother's hand.
Together they went to school.

lunch   clothes   stuffed
                                animal

Daniel was afraid to go into the
big classroom. He peeked inside.
He didn't know any of the children.
"Let's go in," said Daniel's mother.

"Don't go," said Daniel.
She bent down and kissed him.
"Don't go," Daniel whispered again.

The teacher came over and gave Daniel a nametag.

"Hi, Daniel. Remember me? I'm Mr. Berry."

He wore a nametag, too.

"Would you like to go to the water table?"

Daniel shook his head no.

"How about building with blocks?"

Daniel looked down at the floor.

"What about a story?"

Daniel hid behind his mother as
the other children went to sit on
the story rug with Mr. Berry.
Tears rolled down Daniel's cheeks.
"Don't go!"

Daniel's mother put her arms all around him.
Then she led him to a cubby that had his name on it.
She tucked a photo of her and Daniel on the shelf
and placed it right next to his blanket and Dog.
"Dog is safe and sound," she said, smiling.

Daniel snuggled closer. "Are you coming back?"
She whispered in his ear, "Oh, Daniel,
I will always come back to you. Always."
Daniel nodded, but his lower lip trembled.
"Let's do our special good-bye," she added.

Daniel and his mother did their eyelash kiss.
Daniel giggled. Her long lashes tickled his.

Mr. Berry gently took Daniel's hand
and led him to the story rug.
A boy wearing a baseball cap just like his
moved over so Daniel could sit down.
Next to Daniel was a girl who smiled.

Mr. Berry began to sing a song and tell a story.
Daniel's mother listened at the door.

When the story was over, the girl tapped Daniel
on the arm. "Let's go to the water table," she said.
"Can I come, too?" asked the boy with the baseball cap.
As they got up, Mr. Berry smiled at them.
He waved good-bye to Daniel's mother.

She waved back.
Daniel didn't smile,
but he waved good-bye, too.

Then he went over to the water table
with his two new friends.
When he looked up,
his mother was gone.

"My name is Marisol," said the girl.
"My name is Gavin," said the boy.
"My name is Daniel," said Daniel.
They got so wet they had to change their clothes.

Then everyone went outside to the sandbox.
They played on the swings in the playground
and picked up leaves for the class bulletin board.

When the class came inside, they made pumpkin cookies.
The air smelled of ginger while they cleaned up.
Daniel's stomach began to grumble. Loud.
Marisol heard it growl. "I'm hungry, too," she said.
Gavin said, "So am I."

Luckily, just then Mr. Berry called, "Lunch!"
Everyone ate their lunches from home
and saved the pumpkin cookies for last.

After lunch it was naptime, but Daniel wasn't tired.
Mr. Berry covered him with the blanket
he had brought from home.
Daniel thought of his mother and got very sad.
He wanted his stuffed dog,
so he tiptoed over to his cubby.
He found the photo of him and
his mother and put it in his pocket.

Daniel cuddled with Dog under the blanket.
Dog smelled like home.
His fur tickled Marisol's nose
as she lay on the mat next to Daniel's.
She began to giggle. Then Gavin giggled.
Soon everybody was giggling.
Even Daniel started to laugh.
No one was sleepy. Except Mr. Berry.

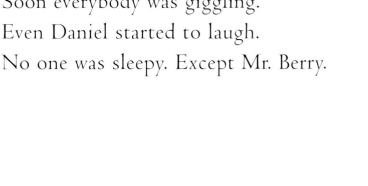

"I guess naptime's over," Mr. Berry said, laughing.
Daniel put Dog close by on the puppet stage.

Then he sat next to Marisol and Gavin and they
all drew pictures about their first day at school.
They shared every crayon.
Daniel looked out the window.

Parents started to pick up their children.
Marisol hugged her grandmother.
"See you tomorrow," said Marisol.

Gavin was excited to see his father.
"Bye, Daniel!" he said as he waved.
Daniel watched the door for his mother's face.

When Daniel saw her,
he ran to her with open arms.
"How was your day?" she asked him.
"Dog had fun," said Daniel.

As they walked down the hall together,
Daniel said, "Wait. Don't go!"
He ran back to his classroom.
"This is for you, Mommy."

Daniel and his mother went home
carrying the picture of Daniel's first day
and two extra pumpkin cookies.

Checklist for First Day at Preschool

Here are some things you'll want to pack for your child:

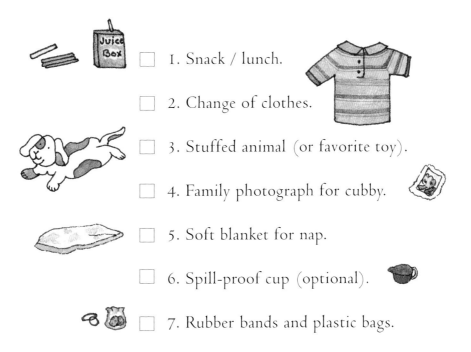

- ☐ 1. Snack / lunch.
- ☐ 2. Change of clothes.
- ☐ 3. Stuffed animal (or favorite toy).
- ☐ 4. Family photograph for cubby.
- ☐ 5. Soft blanket for nap.
- ☐ 6. Spill-proof cup (optional).
- ☐ 7. Rubber bands and plastic bags.

Note: Keep rubber bands and plastic bags handy. They make it easier to take home artwork and baked goods. Daniel's mom rolled up his drawing and secured it with a rubber band, and she put the pumpkin cookies in a plastic bag.

Getting Ready for Preschool

A Note from the Editor

The day my son started preschool I was a wreck. After having a babysitter all to himself for the past three years, how would he survive without one-on-one attention from a caregiver? How would this free-spirited, headstrong child adjust to the rules and standards of a classroom? When we arrived at school that first day, I put his things in his brand-new cubby and prepared myself for a dramatic and tearful good-bye. To my astonishment, my son went right over to a table where several children were putting puzzles together, smiled at me, and said, "You can go to work now, Mommy."

If only every good-bye were that easy! Of course, we all know that's not the case, and often the separation process can be painful and scary for children *and* parents. That's why it's important to say good-bye the right way. In *Don't Go!* Daniel's mom spends time in the classroom, making sure that he is comfortable before she leaves. Don't rush your good-bye or try to sneak out of the room when your child's not looking. It's also important to tell your child that you will always come back.

Here are some tips to help you and your child get ready for the big day:

1. If your child's preschool doesn't automatically set up a home visit with the teacher prior to the start of school, try to arrange one so that he or she can meet your child ahead of time and so that you can discuss any concerns with the teacher. Make sure you have a system set up with the teacher for communicating about your child's adjustment during the first weeks of school.
2. Not every child is ready for a full day of school the very first day, so arrange for a more gradual phase-in during the first week if you feel your child may need it. You may wish to stay close to the classroom the first few days in case your child needs you.
3. Make getting ready for school a project you and your child can share. Go through the family album together and ask your child to pick out some favorite pictures of home to keep in his or her cubby.

As a fellow parent, the best advice I can offer is simply that you should give loads of love and reassurance to your child during this transitional period. It is from this safe and secure place that our children make their first wobbly steps toward independence.

Michele Coppola

Daniel's Pumpkin Vanilla-Chip Cookies

These are Daniel's favorite fall cookies. They are so moist and chewy that they can last well over a week when packed in a tin container. They are fun for a child to make with the help of a grownup. If you'd rather not have nuts in your cookies, substitute ½ cup of chocolate morsels for the chopped walnuts and omit the top decorations.

Ingredients

¾ cup (1½ sticks) butter, room temperature

8-ounce package cream cheese, softened

1 cup packed light-brown sugar

⅔ cup granulated sugar

2 teaspoons vanilla extract

1 extra-large egg, beaten

1 teaspoon ground nutmeg

¼ teaspoon ground ginger

1½ cups pumpkin puree, canned or cooked

2 cups sifted unbleached flour

1 teaspoon baking powder

½ cup chopped walnuts (optional)

½ cup pitted dates, chopped

12-ounce bag white-chocolate morsels

Whole blanched almonds or pecan halves to
     decorate top of each cookie

Tools

Measuring cups, measuring spoons, electric mixer, large mixing bowl, small bowl, cookie sheets, parchment paper, spatula, wire cookie rack, airtight tins, aprons, dishtowels, and oven mitts.

Directions

1. Preheat the oven to 375 degrees.
2. In a large bowl, with an electric mixer, beat the butter, cream cheese, sugars, and vanilla until the mixture is smooth.
3. Add the egg, spices, and pumpkin. Beat until thoroughly blended.
4. In a separate bowl, sift the flour and baking powder together. Add to the wet mixture, and beat on low speed just until blended.
5. Slowly pour in the walnuts, dates, and chocolate morsels. Stir.
6. When the dough is mixed, grease a cookie sheet or line with parchment paper. Drop teaspoonfuls of dough 2 inches apart on each sheet.
7. Put one almond or pecan half on top of each cookie.
8. Bake 15–20 minutes until slightly brown at edges. Cool on sheet or rack for 2 minutes. They can later be stored in an airtight tin.

Yield: 8 dozen 2-inch cookies